This book belongs to

Megan WELLS

Dora's READY-TO-READ Adventures

Based on the TV series *Dora the Explorer*® as seen on Nick Jr.®

SIMON SPOTLIGHT
An imprint of Simon & Schuster Children's Publishing Division
1230 Avenue of the Americas, New York, New York 10020
Dora's Picnic; Follow Those Feet!; and *Dora in the Deep Sea* © 2003
Viacom International Inc. *I Love My Papi!* and *Say "Cheese!"* © 2004
Viacom International Inc. All rights reserved.
NICKELODEON, NICK JR., *Dora the Explorer,* and all related titles, logos, and
characters are registered trademarks of Viacom International Inc.
All rights reserved, including the right of reproduction in
whole or in part in any form.
SIMON SPOTLIGHT, READY-TO-READ, and colophon are registered
trademarks of Simon & Schuster, Inc.
Manufactured in the United States of America
First Edition
2 4 6 8 10 9 7 5 3 1
ISBN 0-689-87815-X
These titles were previously published individually by Simon Spotlight.
These titles were previously catalogued individually by the Library of Congress.

Dora's READY-TO-READ Adventures

Ready-to-Read

Simon Spotlight/Nick Jr.

New York   London   Toronto   Sydney

Contents

Dora's Picnic

by Christine Ricci   illustrated by Susan Hall

Hi! I am  **DORA**. We are going to a picnic at Play Park! Play Park has a  **SLIDE**, a **SANDBOX**, and **SWINGS**.

9

My **mami** is helping me
make  -and-
PEANUT-BUTTER   JELLY
sandwiches for the picnic.

10

 **is my best friend.**

BOOTS

He loves 🍌**!**

BANANAS

 **BOOTS** has a bunch of  **BANANAS** for the picnic.

 is riding his  to the picnic.

BENNY

BICYCLE

14

He is carrying  juice

APPLE

in his .

BASKET

Here comes the  .

BIG RED CHICKEN

The  has a big  of

BIG RED CHICKEN

BAG

for the picnic.

POPCORN

Yummy!

Look!  BABY BLUE BIRD has a bowl of fruit in her  WAGON .

The fruit bowl has ,

BANANAS

, and .

APPLES   **GRAPES**

19

What did  **TICO** bring to the picnic?

 **brought**  .

TICO   BREAD

The 🍞 **is filled with**

BREAD

🫐 **and** 🥜 **!**

BLUEBERRIES   NUTS

 **ISA** made  **CUPCAKES** to share with everyone.

I like chocolate  CUPCAKES

with PINK icing. What kind

do you like?

Look out for  SWIPER.
He will try to swipe
the food we brought.

 is hiding behind

the 🌳 .

TREE

Say, "Swiper, no swiping!"

Yay! You stopped 🦝 !

SWIPER

We made it to Play Park! This  is perfect for our picnic. But first we want to play!

TABLE

 **TICO** **likes to go down the** . **SLIDE**

 **is making a**

BABY BLUE BIRD   SAND CASTLE

in the  **.**

SANDBOX

28

The  pushes

BIG RED CHICKEN   BOOTS

and  on the .

ISA   SWINGS

29

This is the best picnic!
We can all share the food.
What would **you** bring
to a picnic?

Follow Those Feet!

by Christine Ricci   illustrated by Susan Hall

Hi! I am .
DORA  **BOOTS** and I found

some  in the .
FOOTPRINTS **SANDBOX**

I wonder who made them.

Do you know?

33

Did I make these ?

FOOTPRINTS

No, my feet are small.
I did not make these .

FOOTPRINTS

Did  make these ?
BOOTS   FOOTPRINTS

No, his are shaped
FOOTPRINTS

like an oval. He did not

make these .
FOOTPRINTS

Who made these ?

FOOTPRINTS

We can follow them to find out.

Hello,  !
BIG RED CHICKEN

Did you make these ?
FOOTPRINTS

No, his feet have three
toes! He did not make
these .

FOOTPRINTS

Did the  make

HORSE

these 👣?

FOOTPRINTS

No, the horse wears  HORSESHOES on her feet. She did not make these FOOTPRINTS.

41

Did the  make these footprints?

CROCODILE

No, the  CROCODILE has long nails. He did not make these FOOTPRINTS.

43

Did the  make the ?
RABBIT   FOOTPRINTS

No, she has two long feet

and two short feet.

She did not make these

FOOTPRINTS

Did the  SNAKE make these  FOOTPRINTS ? No, the  SNAKE does not have feet!

He slides across the ground. He did not make these .

FOOTPRINTS

Do you see ? Did

SWIPER   SWIPER

make these ?

FOOTPRINTS

No, 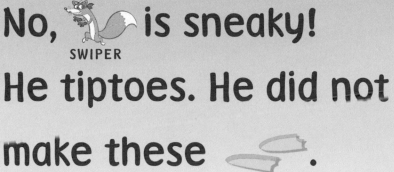 is sneaky!
SWIPER

He tiptoes. He did not

make these 👣.
FOOTPRINTS

The  go all the way to
FOOTPRINTS
the beach!

They go by the
SHELLS

toward the  .
SAND CASTLE

Now do you know who
made these  ?
FOOTPRINTS

It was **BENNY**! He walked to the beach in his new **FLIPPERS**!

Yay! We did it! We found
out who made the !
FOOTPRINTS

Dora in the Deep Sea

by Christine Ricci   illustrated by Robert Roper

Hi! I am  . This is .

DORA

BOOTS

And here is our friend,

.  looks sad.

PIRATE PIG

PIRATE PIG

What is wrong,  ?

PIRATE PIG

"I have lost my  !"

TREASURE CHEST

says  . "The

PIRATE PIG   TREASURE CHEST

fell off my  and

SHIP

into the  !"

SEA

58

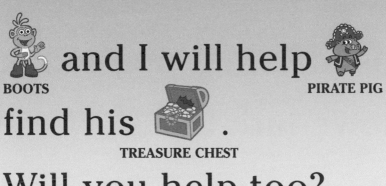 and I will help **PIRATE PIG**

find his  .

TREASURE CHEST

Will you help too?

We need something to take
us down into the  .
SEA

What can take us into the

SEA ?

60

A  can take us down

SUBMARINE

into the  !

SEA

Ooh, we are going down into the  .
SEA

Look! A 🏰 !
SAND CASTLE

Hello, 🦀 !
KING CRAB

63

There is a 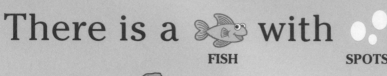 with
FISH   SPOTS
by the 🪨 .
ROCK

I see a 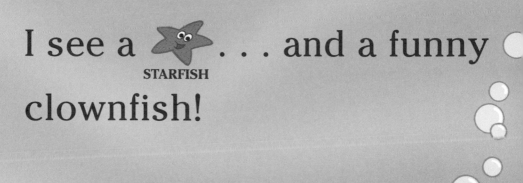 STARFISH . . . and a funny clownfish!

Boots spots a  .
GREEN TURTLE

Pirate Pig sees .
YELLOW SEA HORSES

66

Oh, no! Here come some
 !
LOBSTERS

They will try to pinch

the  with their !
SUBMARINE   **CLAWS**

We drove the
SUBMARINE
past the  !
LOBSTERS
Now we need to find
the  .
TREASURE CHEST

Hooray! We found the  !

TREASURE CHEST

But we have to watch out for  .

SWIPER

He will try to swipe

the .

TREASURE CHEST

73

Do you see ?

SWIPER

Look! 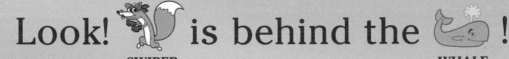 **SWIPER** is behind the 🐳 ! **WHALE**

He is going to swipe

the 📦 ! **TREASURE CHEST**

We have to say "  , no swiping!"

You helped us stop !

Yay! 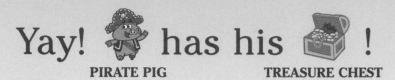 has his  !

PIRATE PIG **TREASURE CHEST**

Thank you for helping!

I Love My Papi!

by Alison Inches   illustrated by Dave Aikins

My PAPI and I love to do things together!

 **PAPI** **taught me a super soccer kick. Look, I kicked the**  **into the** **!**

SOCCER BALL

GOAL

We also love playing .
BASEBALL
coaches my team.
PAPI

He taught us how to swing the  BAT and slide into home BASE.

On weekends  and I
PAPI
ride BIKES together.

Or sail on a .
BOAT

Sometimes we go to the 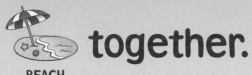 together.

BEACH

We build giant  and
SAND CASTLES

play in the .
WAVES

My  is a really good .

PAPI COOK

He taught me how to bake a special  and make

CAKE

yummy .

SANDWICHES

90

Sometimes we pack a  PICNIC

and share it with my

friend .
BOOTS

My  made us this
PAPI

swing! He can build

anything with .
TOOLS

TIRE

94

One time  took us to
the 🎪 . 🐵 loved the 🤡 .

PAPI

CIRCUS   BOOTS   CLOWNS

Then  bought us  and

PAPI POPCORN

 for a treat.

STRAWBERRY ICE CREAM

Yum! Yum!

At the end of every day  tucks me into .

PAPI

BED

Then we read a  .
BOOK
I like ▥▥ about 🐄🐑 .
BOOKS   ANIMALS

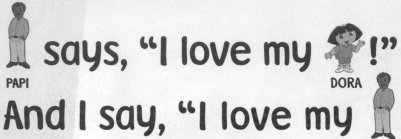 says, "I love my !"

PAPI
DORA

And I say, "I love my !"

PAPI

NICK JR.

DORA the EXPLORER

Say "Cheese!"

by Christine Ricci   illustrated by Steven Savitsky

Hi! I am  (DORA). My friend (BOOTS)
is sick today.

How can we cheer him up?

I know! We can visit  BOOTS

at his  TREE HOUSE.

And we can use my  CAMERA

to take pictures of things

 BOOTS likes.

 **BOOTS** would love a picture

of  **BACKPACK** and  **MAP**.

Say "  **CHEESE** !"

We are at 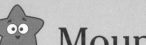 Mountain.
STAR
 Mountain is filled
STAR
with  .
STARS
 loves to play with
BOOTS
the  !
STARS

Look! There is  .

 has all kinds of  .

Say "  !"

Here is a fruit garden.

Which fruit does  like?

Yes,  loves !

BOOTS

BANANAS

Who else loves 🍌?

BANANAS

The 🦉!

BIRD

Say "🧀!"

CHEESE

 likes silly things too!
BOOTS

The  are making silly
CROCODILES

faces.

Ha, ha, ha! Smile,  !

CROCODILES

Say "  !"

CHEESE

Do you see more silly things?

113

 has baked a

ISA   CAKE

for  .

BOOTS

Yummy!

 made a  for  .

BENNY CARD BOOTS

 and  look at

ISA BENNY

the  .

CAMERA

Say " ! "

CHEESE

 likes to swing

through the .

 likes to swing

through the  too!

BABY JAGUAR likes to play

in the FLOWERS.

Say "CHEESE!"

Here is an  cart.
ICE-CREAM

 loves  !
BOOTS   ICE CREAM

Say "  !"
CHEESE

118

Uh-oh. Do you see someone behind the  cart?

ICE-CREAM

It is !
SWIPER

 wants to swipe
SWIPER

our .
CAMERA

120

We have to stop  SWIPER.

Say " SWIPER, no swiping!"

Yay! We stopped !
SWIPER

Hey, there is !
TICO

 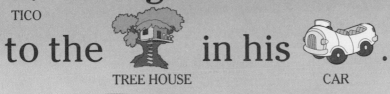 will give us a ride

TICO

to the  in his .

TREE HOUSE   CAR

Say "  !"

CHEESE

123

Hooray! We made it to the .

TREE HOUSE

And  loves all the

BOOTS

pictures!

We cheered up .

BOOTS

Thanks for helping!

Oh, I have to take **1**
ONE

more picture.
 wants a picture of
BOOTS

you!

Say "  !"
CHEESE